THE FART BOOK

THE DISGUSTING ADVENTURES OF MILO SNOTROCKET

J. B. O'NEIL

Sky Pony Press
New York

Sky Pony Press books may be purchased in bulk at special discounts for sales promotion, corporate gifts, fund-raising, or educational purposes. Special editions can also be created to specifications. For details, contact the Special Sales Department, Sky Pony Press, 307 West 36th Street, 11th Floor, New York, NY 10018 or info@skyhorsepublishing.com.

Sky Pony® is a registered trademark of Skyhorse Publishing, Inc.®, a Delaware corporation.

Visit our website at www.skyponypress.com.

10 9 8 7 6 5 4 3 2 1

Library of Congress Cataloging-in-Publication Data is available on file.

Cover design by Michael Short
Cover and interior illustrations by J. B. O'Neil

Print ISBN: 978-1-5107-2434-1
Ebook ISBN: 978-1-5107-2436-5

Printed in Canada

TABLE OF CONTENTS

DISCLAIMER:
THIS BOOK IS
INTENDED FOR HUMOR
ONLY. PLEASE DO NOT
TRY ANY OF THIS
AT HOME.

THE SIDESHOT

FART

My name is Milo Snotrocket, and I consider myself to be one of the true experts in the world in the art of the fart. I've dedicated all ten years of my life to researching every single one of them, so that the human race can better understand the true power of this important weapon and use it in the most effective way possible. You can think of the book that you now hold in your hands as the *Encyclopedia Fart-Tannica* of all farts known to man.

If you're one of those lucky people with a natural talent for butt whistling (as I suspect you are), or if you consider yourself the maestro of a one-kid, gassy, grumbling orchestra, you're probably familiar with the classic Sideshot fart. It happens to be one of the simplest and easiest farts in the world to perform because just about any backdoor breezy dabbler can do it. And whether you're an amateur bottom-burper or a super-advanced, expert bean-blower, I'm sure you've noticed this classic fart being deployed. Maybe it was the old man sitting on a park bench feeding the pigeons, or the kid who sits in front of you at school.

Just about anyone can perfect the Sideshot in two simple steps. Step one: prepare your body for maximum airflow. All you have to do is tilt one hip to the side like you're about to tip over. Step two: simply unclench your butt cheeks and let it all go, faster than a speeding spit wad!

For a nice clean shot, I recommend aiming your gas attack at a forty-five-degree angle. By the way, this fart happens to be how I met one of my best friends, Farty McPhee. I spotted him letting loose with the Sideshot on the seesaw (not as easy as you'd imagine) and knew I'd found my partner in slime.

THE SKIPPING STONE

On a gorgeous spring day, when the grass is swaying and the birds are singing in the trees, you might decide to take a walk down to the lake, sit down under a tree, and enjoy the perfect weather. If you're super quiet and listen very carefully, you might hear a little grumbling in your tummy. And if no one is around except the frogs in the bushes and the slugs dragging their slimy shells through the grass, and you are all one with nature, you'll take a deep breath and know it's time for the Skipping Stone.

That's right, in the middle of all the outdoor sights and sounds and smells, you'll want to throw in your own airy chimes. Go ahead. Clench and release. It might sound like a stone skipping on water: like *hoppity-hoppity-hop-kerplunk*! Or more like birdsong: *Chirp-chirp-chirp-tweeeeeeeet.*

The key to the Skipping Stone is to let it sing. Listen to your butt chimes work their magic. It's all natural. It's your gift to the world. This windy ripple fart will make you feel much closer to Mother Nature. Best of all, it's 100 percent bio-degradable, which means that you don't have to worry about damaging the ozone layer with this methane miracle.

MORSE CODE

This is a top secret farting method for super sleuths and spies; it's not for the amateur, I assure you. This is serious stuff to be deployed only for the flatulent elite. Learning to intercept and send your own Morse code messages vapor style is like joining a secret club. It isn't easy, and it'll take a whole lot of practice to get it right. But when you do, you'll be able to send messages undetected to your friends and fellow Morse flatulators without ever getting caught.

For example, *Toot-toooot-tooooot. Toot! Too-toot. Toot-tooooo-toot. Toooot-too-toot* is "weird" in fartspeak. Practice this with someone you trust to share these secrets and adventures with (my buddy Farty McPhee and I are getting pretty good at this). Soon you'll be able to have entire conversations—although you'll want to keep them short—while everyone around you curiously wrinkles their noses and starts walking away. The best part is that all evidence of the message dissolves into thin air and vanishes into unknowing nostrils without a trace.

THE ROCKET SHIP

Forget about gravity. Forget roller coasters. Forget tornadoes. Twisters will seem like dust mites compared to this rocket-shooting methane canon fart.

The Rocket Ship is strong enough to send you not only flying out of your chair, but floating through space on a powerful gas propeller (although most of the time you'll stop short of the ozone layer). It might send you blasting up from your treehouse to the top of a nearby water tower or the Empire State Building in New York.

When you feel it rumbling in your tummy, ready to take off, act quickly and strap a parachute onto your back because you're in for the ride of your life. If you're an exceptional farter, you might even get across the Pacific. Say "goodbye, Earth!" and "Hello, Sky!"

The single recorded incident of the Rocket Ship that broke the atmospheric barrier was by an unusually hungry boy of eight who was obsessed with chili, black beans, and burritos. After his fifth meal of the day and about a hundred burps, he closed his eyes, rubbed his belly, and was suddenly launched up, up, and away until he was completely out of sight. If you look up at the sky on cloudless nights, you can still see the glowing gas clouds floating in space.

After that unfortunate incident, parents, teachers, cafeterias, and taco trucks all over the country agreed on a one-burrito-per-day-per-kid rule, which is really a shame if you think about it.

Still, it hasn't stopped the Rocket Ship from happening to bean-loving kids from time to time, all over the world.

THE SCREAM

Have you ever woken up in the middle of the night with an anxious feeling? As though you were jarred awake by a ghost whizzing by or an insect buzzing around in your room while you slept? Or maybe you woke up from a bad dream hearing creepy high-pitched voices? Don't be afraid. Chances are it was just the Scream: a long, loud, extremely high-pitched bottom whistle. It can be pretty alarming if you've never experienced this before, because it doesn't sound anything like your average bottom burp.

This fart really belongs in a horror movie for its ability to produce blood-curdling sound effects, because it'll make your skin crawl. To actual ghosts, it sounds like nails on a chalkboard. In fact, if you want to scare away potential monsters lurking in the shadows, you may want to let out an ear-piercing Scream fart. It's also the perfect weapon to ward off bullies and boring teachers. When in danger (or just to get out of the classroom for a minute), stink things up with a Screamer.

THE SPUTTER

When a car's engine sputters out, you take it to the garage so the mechanic can have a look. When a fart sputters out, you give your compliments to the chef. In some cultures, the polite thing to do is burp after a meal. In the same way, according to the *Fart Etiquette Manual* published by the International Society of Flatulence Enthusiasts (of which I am a lifetime member), farting can be seen as a similar gesture of appreciation. It's like applause for a job well done, a meal enjoyed.

The Sputter always starts strong, with great thunderous bugle sounds of appreciation. After that, like all applause, it quietly fades away into a series of butt chuckles and hiccups. That's right, even the lingering scent of a grateful fart must fade—gone but not forgotten.

THE EXPLOSION

Ever felt the earth rumbling beneath your feet? Well, with all the crazy news on television about natural disasters these days, you probably thought it was an earthquake. But here's the truth (and I know scientists will back me up on this): 99 percent of all reported earthquakes are just the beginning of an enormous, gargantuan, humongous fart called "The Explosion" that's starting somewhere nearby . . . maybe even in your own butt!

Here's how the Explosion happens: First your bottom starts to tingle, then your tummy starts to grumble, your toes start to tremble, and your chair or the floor under your feet begins to groan. Like thunder before a storm, that's when you know a "big one" is coming.

Your first reaction will be to take cover, but there's really nowhere to hide from this mother of all farts. Your second impulse will be to run for the bathroom, but don't bother because you'll probably blow out the walls with this huge explosion. In my own expert opinion, there's only one thing that you can do: just let it happen. Plant both feet on the ground, get into superhero stance, close your eyes, and unleash this earthshaking whopper of natural gas.

THE VIBRATO

I bet you know someone who loves classical music. Maybe it's that kid in seventh grade that's a whiz on the tuba, or that man with the deep bass singing voice. Anyway, most kids are familiar with at least a little bit of classical music, even though it's not nearly as popular these days as, well, *real* music like heavy metal. The thing that makes it classical, though, is its timeless appeal. And that's exactly what makes the Vibrato fart such a classic and inspired choice for auditions on those special occasions.

People who've heard the intense beauty of this musical farting selection will never forget this irresistible ear candy. It's been known to make grown men cry, and sooth the savage soul of wild gorillas. It also happens to smell really bad.

The Vibrato is definitely one of the more artistic and unforgettable ways to break wind. Maybe they'll let you into your school band as a soloist after they hear your first performance. But even if they don't, make sure to keep in practice with this one so you can impress your grandma with a song the next time she visits.

POPCORN FARTING

No, you don't need a microwave the size of a refrigerator to add the popcorn variety to your list of gassy triumphs. All you need is great butt reflexes and a whole lot of wind. The Popcorn fart requires a LOT of control and stamina because it always comes in a lightning-fast sequence of bottom pops. Have you ever heard of just one kernel of popcorn popping? Me neither. And that's why you'll need to have split-second butt reflexes ready in order to pull this one off in a convincing way.

Also known as the "Machine Gun," this is one of the most fun and impressive fart techniques ever invented. Use it to play cops and robbers or to drive away skunks and other creatures you don't want rummaging through your trash or sneaking around in your backyard.

PEANUT BUTTER FARTS

THBTTT

You're a good kid. You wouldn't hurt a fly. Or maybe just a fly, and the occasional slug. But how do you get back at the school bully while maintaining your squeaky clean reputation for being an all-around awesome peacekeeping fifth grader? Weaponized farts in a jar are the answer. Please note: You'll have to eat a lot of PB&J sandwiches for lunch to make this work, but don't worry: it'll be well worth it. Here's how this works:

- Step 1: Save a whole bunch of different-sized peanut butter jars to keep your farts in.
- Step 2: Open a jar, bend over, and let 'er rip!
- Step 3: Close the top quick, and stash three or four in your backpack in case of emergencies.

If you find yourself in a sticky situation with the school bully, just take the jar out and unleash the magic poo perfume. You'll have him either running away in disgust or completely stunned into submission by your smelly peanut butter potion.

THE STRONG, SILENT TYPE

SSSSSS

I heard some ladies on TV once talk about how much they supposedly love guys like this, but if you test this one out with the girls at school, you'll soon figure out this just isn't the case. Not with the strong, silent fart, anyway. This fart is known for its extremely strong "won't-hear-it-coming" fragrance, which just sneaks up on you with no warning whatsoever. While other farts announce their stinkiness with a long honk (or at least a soft squeal), the strong, silent type just fills the room with its smelly presence. It travels fast, too, and leaves everyone wondering "where the heck did that stink bomb come from?"

This is the best fart for people who like to multitask. Here's why: you can be pretending to do your homework in biology class, giving your little brother a wedgie, or playing a video game with your Dad, while at the same time secretly preparing for just the right moment to let this devastating sneak attack out of your butt.

When you finally do let it go with a silent sizzle, you just wrinkle your nose, shake your head, and say to the person sitting beside you, "Do you mind?" as if it was their idea in the first place. And of course, the strong, silent type's origins will remain a mystery forever to those unlucky enough to be in the same room and fall victim to it.

THE ROTTEN EGG CLOUD

The Rotten Egg Cloud is an unmistakable fart phenomenon. Why? Because it smells like rotten eggs boiled in expired milk until they explode in a nasty mess. But the milky-sour, rotten egg stench is not the most distinct feature of this particular fart. It's the way it moves around the room and tickles the nostrils of everyone who gets in its path.

Technically, I classify this fart as a "cloud" because it's an inescapable vapor that just kind of hangs in the air and follows your innocent victims around like a rain cloud. It also sticks to your clothes for hours, and there's absolutely nothing you can do to avoid it. You definitely don't want to get caught in this cloud like a plane gets caught in atmospheric turbulence. Even expert bottom-blasters pinch their noses for this one, and the only thing you can do to save yourself is to hold your breath.

POO PERFUME

Wear this rare human concoction and you'll be sure to attract every stray dog in the neighborhood (as well as incredibly dirty looks from passing strangers). One whiff will send the average person reeling and scampering around for almost anything they can find to offset the stink factor of this Poo Perfume: whether it's bouquet of roses, or even a dirty old fish bowl. And be forewarned: don't wear too much of it unless you want people to grimace and faint at the first sniff of you.

This horrible fragrance is in high demand all over the world because the bottling process requires a lot of time and care, and only the stinkiest, smelliest farts are used to extract the essence of Poo Perfume. I know for a fact that the President of the local chapter of the International Society of Fart Enthusiasts wears just a hint of this perfume to our quarterly meetings where we discuss cutting-edge farting techniques and breakthroughs in backfiring vapors.

THE PARTY POOPER

Bfffft

Make sure your grandma has her smelling salts before you unleash this one, because the Party Pooper is not for the faint of heart or the unprepared.

This festive stink torpedo goes off like a firework and is perfect for large gatherings, where it's guaranteed to blow party hats clean off people's heads. You can catch your guests off guard right as they are bobbing their heads to a catchy tune, busting a move on the dance floor, or talking to somebody at the punch bowl. In fact, this is one party favor that never goes unnoticed—loud and stinky with perfect timing.

At your next birthday celebration, consider whipping out this fun little pants-ripper when you blow out the candles on your birthday cake. Because who the heck wants to see a dumb clown at your party anyway? This hilarious fart is sure to turn heads and make the farter the life of the party, especially if you surprise everyone in the middle of a game of musical chairs after the music stops.

THE RED ALERT

Have you ever been in the middle of a scene in the school play, or stuck in the car on the highway miles from the nearest rest stop and felt a Red Alert fart well up inside you? It grumble-grumbles and chews at your stomach, and you know it'll go off any second. And it does—like a long, loud siren.

That's right, at the most inconvenient time possible, the Red Alert will say "howdy pardner!" and demand your immediate attention. And even if you're stuck in the middle of a midterm exam in Latin class, be sure to get yourself up and your poop-chute to the bathroom as fast as you can, or else you'll be reduced to a whimpering baby in need of a diaper-changing. This threatening warning fart will make you feel like good old fiber is not your friend, and make you wish your mom hadn't made you eat those prunes with your cereal that morning. Again, the Red Alert represents a real emergency.

Run—don't walk—to the closest toilet, and take care of business.

THE BOTTLE CAP

The Bottle Cap, which almost always pops out of your butt when you twist to the right, is a personal favorite of line dancers and hula-hoop champions alike. It's hard to perform this one perfectly, but with a little practice you'll be able to bust this move and blast those fart fumes to the rhythm in no time.

The first step to doing this right is putting on some appropriate music. If you asked your grandma, she might recommend "Do the Twist," "Twist and Shout," and "Twisting the Night Away" to get maximum squeezing pressure for this fun little fart (don't worry, your grandma's been performing the Bottle Cap since *waaay* before you were born). Ask your mom, and she'll probably tell you that she danced to "Achy, Breaky Farts" during her Bottle Cap days as a girl. But really, the song's up to you. Anything that's upbeat, jiggly, and wiggly will do as long as it's fun and there's lots of general right-twisting involved.

If this is your first time performing the Bottle Cap, start off with some stretches to warm up. Then spread your arms, jump around, throw your hands in the air, wiggle your fingers, and swish your feet. Keep your elbows in and knees a little bent, and start moving your hips from side to side. Then quickly twist to the right, and *POP*! You've just performed your first Bottle Cap fart (and I bet it won't be your last).

THE RATTLE SNAKE

The Rattle Snake fart is 100 percent pure, nasty stink juice. It'll make you cover your nose and say "Pee-yoo! Is that poison? Is that rotten dog food, or some kind of horrible science lab accident? Did something crawl under the floorboards and die?"

At our last meeting, the President of the International Society of Fart Enthusiasts did a demonstration of the Rattle Snake fart, and the sound of the sputtering vapor venom that shot out of his rear end lasted all of eight minutes, which he told us was a new world record. The smell actually stuck around much longer, and we got complaints from the maintenance crew.

I wanted to try it out myself, and after several attempts (and a lot of wasted gas trying to get it right), I finally did it! I didn't tell my mom about it, and it drove her absolutely bonkers trying to figure out what the heck that smell was. She kept looking out the window and under the furniture, worried she might have to call an exterminator. And when she found out that it was just my butt, she was pretty mad and told me to go play outside for three hours.

THE STIRRER

I gotta admit, the Stirrer always gives me a stomach ache. It usually starts at night after I've watched a documentary on TV about hurricanes or tornadoes. My stomach usually continues where the TV show ended and starts to brew its own little twister, putting everything I ate that day—scrambled eggs, cheese whip, pretzels, and Mom's meatloaf—through a gassy blender.

To make matters worse, when I go to bed with a Stirrer fart bubbling around in my belly, I always seem to have dreams of blenders blending really gross things together, like mushy bananas, pickle juice, hair balls, vanilla yogurt, ketchup globs, and celery sticks—things you do not want rolling around in your stomach. To top it off, the next morning I usually end up watching my mom make one of her all-natural, healthy smoothies—carrot juice with a spoonful of cod liver oil for a glowing complexion—and typically feel like hurling all over the breakfast table. The Stirrer swirls around in my stomach, threatening to blow, but I perform a quick side-shot to let all that pressure out of my body. Disaster averted . . . until next time they start showing "Tornado Week" on TV!

THE COUGH COVER-UP

If you don't want anyone to hear your fart, for whatever reason, here's what I do: distract them with a really loud cough to mask it. That's right, whether you're waiting to be called into the principal's office or in the middle of a silent study hall, the art of the Cough Cover-Up fart can really come in handy. Here's an example: my homeroom teacher started calling me a "farting menace" in class and so I've lost all fart privileges for the first period of school.

Actually, come to think of it . . . I've lost my farting privileges in every class in school. But here's the beautiful thing about the Cough Cover-Up fart: there's no limit to how many times I can cough! Or sneeze. Or burp. You'd be amazed at how much gas a ten-year-old boy can unleash on the world and still be able to keep it a secret from every grown-up on the planet.

What really gets to me, though, is that I can't always claim my proudest farts—my cafeteria slush-inspired, mega-explosion farts that happen to come to me in the classroom right after lunch, usually when I'm working on multiplication tables. Of course, even with the Cough Cover-Up, when the vinegar-scented gas starts spreading around the room, the other students look at me with both disgust and admiration. And I just have to smile.

THE AFTER-FART

The After-Fart is the curtain call of farts, the encore, and the hand shooting up from the grave in the last scene of that creepy zombie movie. It always is a spine-tingling surprise for me, while at the same time it's extremely revolting for everybody else in the room. As if my rotten eggs soaked in vinegar whiff-and-sniff cloud were not enough, the After-Fart tops it off with a loud walloping stink-steamer. Long story short, the After-Fart is the exclamation point of all farts!

I read in history class that some of the greatest public speakers of all time have used them to make a point, so when I was running for class president and had to make a speech, I made sure to blow some huge After-Farts to follow my best points.

"Vote for me, and I'll put a whoopee cushion on every seat in the cafeteria!" *Plooooot.*

"No school on Fridays!" Double *prooooot.* These farts also come with an overpowering odor that you won't soon forget—a mix of poo and dirty gym socks. If you enjoy having the last laugh (or the last word), the After-Fart would be your pooplet puff of choice. Use it wisely.

THE DUET

OK, so the Duet comes in two forms. If you're a one-kid fart show (like I am most of the time), you can match your favorite musical fart with a deep, froggy burp. Try to get some phlegm in there too to add a croaky texture to the piece. You'll come up with a two-part harmony from both ends of the food chain, which is a really unique sound, in my opinion. That's why I suggested to my music teacher that we add it as a solo for our Christmas program. She just laughed and gave me a pat on the head, but I was being totally serious!

Although, I wasn't too disappointed, because my solo act is nowhere close to as good as my duet featuring my good buddy (and stink-shooter extraordinaire) Farty McPhee. The Duet is our signature song that we perform together, and it's very popular with the playground crowd. Farty does the fart-and-burp, and I do the fart-and-fake-sneeze. Sometimes we throw in some sweat-powered armpit horns in there, too, but our butt horns always steal the show for their stinkiness and originality.

THE SQUIRT

According to the International Society of Fart Enthusiasts, the Squirt is considered to be a "Hall-of-Fame Fart"—not just because it takes the stench scale to ultimate heights, but also because of the color it brings to your life (and underwear). Also known as "The Pant Stainer," "The Mud Duck," and "Gravy Pants," the Squirt definitely leaves its mark in a permanent way. As a result, this particular bottom-shooter is my mom's least favorite fart in my repertoire, and that's really saying something.

Not for the "pop-a-fluffy" dabbler, this stink biscuit is for serious farters only. In fact, it should come with a warning label attached to it that says, "WARNING—THIS FART SHOULD ONLY BE ATTEMPTED BY THE BRAVEST BUTT-BLOWERS ON THE PLANET . . . AND POSSIBLY OTHER PLANETS, TOO."

If an alien ever landed on Earth and demanded to learn the secrets of the Squirt, I'm not even sure I would explain this gooey gift to him. It's too dangerous. However, if he really insisted, and promised not to spread it around to everybody else in the galaxy, I guess I'd have to give him the secret formula:

Prunes + 1 gallon of cottage cheese = Squirts galore.

Knock yourself out, aliens.

THE RACER

VRRROOOM

The Racer revs up, makes a *vrrrooooom* sound, and basically just sets your pants on fire with speed. I use it once in a while when I'm really late for school. It makes me go a whole lot faster than our dinky, old school bus ever could. I can even accelerate just enough to wave at the other kids on the bus as I whiz past.

"How does he do it?" they wonder.

"Does he have a built-in engine on his backpack?"

"Is he on invisible solar-powered roller blades?"

Ha! None of them will guess that I've just let the Racer fart rip, letting me tear up the streets all the way to school with its smooth stinky propeller. That's why I haven't been late for school in three years. I love kicking my shoes up on my desk as I watch all the other kids pile into home room, grumbling and sniffing and scratching their heads. And the mystery of my secret speed remains unsolved.

THE DIRTY ELEVATOR BOMB

Do you know what claustrophobia is? It means "an extreme or irrational fear of confined spaces." While I have no problem with tight spaces, some people are really terrified by the idea of being closed in a room with no way of getting out. Apparently, a fart in an elevator is a claustrophobic person's worst nightmare.

I had to learn this the hard way: I was visiting my dad at his office and riding the elevator up to the eighty-seventh floor of his building when I started to feel a major bubble of poop gas about to burst, so naturally I let it rip. It's not healthy holding in a perfectly good stink torpedo, right? What I didn't know was that the man I was sharing the elevator with was already freaking out about being in the tiny elevator, and my rotten egg cloud drove him over the edge.

His eyes nearly popped out of his head and, believe me, you do not want to see what the back of someone's eyeballs look like, with weird little veins and glazed with shiny eye-goo. He started clawing at the elevator buttons and stumbled out on the next floor. He probably took the stairs after that.

AIRPLANE FARTS

I tell you, nothing feels better than releasing a gargantuan, goosebumps-inducing gas blast at thirty thousand feet. The problem is the other passengers usually don't enjoy it half as much as I do. In fact, there's usually not a lot of pleasure involved on their end of things—just a lot of hyperventilating and deep breathing into the motion sickness bags tucked into that pocket on the back of each seat. Really, they should have some safety information on that sheet that tells people how to react when somebody in the seat in front of you blows a huge fart in your face, which threatens to blast you right out of the aircraft.

Anyway, as I mentioned before, I don't think it's healthy to hold any kind of farts inside your body, if it's telling you that it needs to evacuate. And that's exactly what my body was telling me on this particular airplane, so I had to let it rip. Obviously it smelled like rotten blue cheese until the plane landed four hours later, but here's the really interesting part: When I flew back home a week later with my parents, there was a huge poster of a boy with a fart blasting out of his butt, and a big red "No Farting" sign drawn over it at the airport security desk. And get this: the drawing of the boy looked exactly like me. Coincidence? I'll let you be the judge.

THE BUBBLE-BREWER

Ah, relaxing in the tub after a hard day at school. But wait! Bath time can get a little boring, just lying there in your own dirty bath stuff. I'll admit, it's kinda cool watching your fingers and toes go all wrinkly; it's like you age seventy-seven years in half an hour! But even that gets boring after a while.

Here's an instant cure for bath time boredom: bubbles! That's right, bubbles in your bath make everything better! And heck, if you're really smart, you can combine your new bubble-bath time with the nastiest dinner that your mom makes, which means that if your mom serves up cabbage every Monday, then all you need to do is make Monday night your regular bath night!

Go ahead and fill up the tub with super-steamy water, let all that funky cabbage stew for a couple more minutes in your belly, and then, once you're nice and relaxed in the water . . . it's bubble time! Open up the gates to all that pent-up cabbage gas and fill the tub with thousands of frothy stink bubbles. Who needs to go to some swanky place where they make you put slices of cucumber on your eyes when you've got your own spa right at home?

Note: Make sure that it's just farts coming out of your butt and nothing else!

THE TROUSER BALLOON

This strategy has got to be one of my all-time fart favorites: I call it the "Trouser Balloon."

Here's exactly how it works:

- Step 1: You know those pants with a really tight cuff at the ankle? Wear those. All day. It's even better if they're made of that shiny balloon material.
- Step 2: Eat loads of butt-breaking vegetables and then wait a few hours.
- Step 3: Go out into your back yard, tie a piece of rope around your ankle, and then attach the other end of the rope to something big and heavy, like your garage.
- Step 4: Then start farting, as hard and as heavy as you can.

OK, so here's what will happen if you do all of this correctly: your legs will inflate until you look like the Puff-Rite Marshmallow Man, and you will literally rise up into the sky like a balloon (which is why you need to be tethered to the ground).

This technique is perfect for spying over the next door neighbor's fence. Once you have had enough of all that hanging around, simply pull the waistband out, let the gas escape a little at a time, and float back down to your backyard.

THE WINTER WARMERS

BLAP!

You know how when it's *freeeezing* cold outside and your mom wants you to wear like a hundred scarves, spaceman mittens, and a big ugly down jacket to school? And then she tops it all off by putting three hats on your head, so that you're sweating before you even walk out the door? And then she gets mad when you say you don't want them? I used to hate this stuff every winter, until I discovered this simple mom-fact: They just have no clue that kids come with their very own heating system: HOT FARTS.

Is the icy wind at your back when you're waiting for the school bus? Squeeze out a Winter Warmer and it's like you're standing in front of a fire. Fallen on your butt on the ice? Thaw it out with these hot trots. The best part is that you can even use these stinky superpowers as an act of cold-weather kindness, by dropping one on the seat as you leave so that the next person can sit in warm, cozy comfort.

THE ZIPPER RIPPER

This is a really neat trick, but be advised: it's not one for the amateur. That's because this particular butt bomb requires years of directional farting practice. It may take a little while for you to perfect this technique, but don't worry . . . the results are stink-tacular!

Here's how the Zipper Ripper fart works: by squeezing your butt cheeks *REALLY* hard, it's possible for a sneaky little whiffer to turn around in mid-fart and escape towards the front of your pants instead of taking the usual exit route.

If you can create enough pushing power, this fart can put so much pressure on your zipper that it actually unzips itself! I know this particular fart doesn't serve much purpose, but it's still an impressive trick.

The best part: if you find your hands full when you need to pee, you can easily unzip them without using your hands at all!

THE SKATING RINK STINK

WHOOOSH

The Skating Rink Stink makes you look like the best speed skater in the world!

Here's how it works: First, I eat about three chili dogs at the ice rink concession stand while I'm waiting to for the clerk to find ice skates that fit my feet. Next, I wait for that good old, familiar bubbling feeling in the pit of my tummy. This is my cue to stumble out on onto the ice, and hang on to the side of the rink for dear life (I'm not the strongest skater).

Then, just as I'm about to erupt, I stumble over to the middle of the ice and *Whoooosh*!—a chili-fueled bottom blast sends me speeding off around the rink like a jet-propelled pocket rocket. Best of all, none of the other kids even know what's going on, because all speed skaters stick their butts out anyway!

I swear, I could win the Olympics with this one move. An added benefit to this smelly butt-propulsion technique: as you go shooting across the ice, it'll melt behind you and all the fancy "look-at-me" ice skating kids will fall on their behinds because the rink will be all slushy and gross. Have fun with this one!

MOVIE-THEATER
MOON GAS

I tried this fart for the first time at the premier of the latest *Amazing Fart Man* superhero movie, and it worked like a charm. It's called the Movie-Theater Moon Gas, and if you can time it just right when you're taking a bite of popcorn, nobody will ever even hear it coming before it reaches their unsuspecting nostrils.

This one requires you to slide your butt to the edge of the seat, take a bite of popcorn, and then let rip some silent-but-violent butt bongos. The stink will creep along the floor out of sight, swirling around the other kids' ankles, like a funky fog in a horror film. First, they will feel their legs getting warm, then the smell will hit them, and finally they will look down and see foggy fingers grabbing their feet!

BINGO! They will run screaming from the theater, and you and your buddies will have the whole place to yourselves to finish watching the movie.

THE STICKY STINKY

There are few things more satisfying than dropping an egg bomb out of your butt and someone else getting blamed for it. Well, this fart takes that kind of satisfaction to an entirely new level. It actually *sticks* the stink on to someone else. To do this, you need to build up your supply of sticky butt juice by actually eating a ton of sticky stuff (year-old honey in your mom's pantry is particularly good for this). The next step is to get really close to someone—a crowded hallway between classes at school provides the perfect situation for this.

Once your butt is as close as it can get to your unsuspecting victim (I try to target a clueless substitute teacher whenever possible), let it fly so that the first thing it hits is the other person. The stickiness from the honey will make it stick to their clothes, and that stink will follow them around for the rest of the day! Once you get the hang of this one, you can actually aim for the pocket in their pants so that every time they put their hand in there, it will come out stinking like your back-end blowout!

THE HOT WIND HICCUP

POP   POP   POP

If you ever need a way to get out of a boring class at school, the Hot Wind Hiccup is the fart for you! Here's why this one is particularly effective: There are few things more annoying than hiccups, but they're almost impossible to do deliberately (unlike a burp, which you can do by just swallowing loads of air).

First, you need to be able to squeeze your butt cheeks *REALLY* tightly for this one—in fact the harder you can squeeze, the more effective this one is. Next, force a small amount of gas out about the size of an egg. Because you're clenching your butt cheeks together so tightly, the egg-shaped poot will escape with a little *pop!*, which will make your body jump and create the illusion of a hiccup. Keep doing this at twenty-second intervals, and if necessary, cover your mouth and look around the classroom sheepishly. Other kids will start to giggle, the teacher will turn around to see what's going on, see you "hiccupping," and send you to get a drink of water. Score!

THE BUM-SEN BURNER

Science class. You either love it or you hate it. I usually fall into the "hate it" category, except for when my teacher Mr. Figgins gets out the little gas burners to heat up all kinds of smelly little potions. And boy, can you have fun with those!

Science class is always scheduled after lunch period for me, so I've usually got a belly full of beans or pepperoni pizza sloshing around in my stomach that just can't wait to get out. When Mr. Figgins starts boiling his own concoction of chemicals on top of the Bunsen burner, and the liquids start bubbling faster and faster, my stomach is usually at full boil, too. As soon as he turns his back on the action, it's time to release my human hydrogen bomb right into the boiling beaker of badness. I can usually ignite that innocent little flame and turn it into the school's own version of the volcano known as Twin Buttes, with lethal lava pouring out of the test tubes and oozing down on to the desks. It beats the Mentos and Coke version any day!

RHYTHM AND POOS

This is a great fart for a jam session. Especially when you can't actually play any instruments. The Rhythm and Poos fart will catapult you straight into the spotlight, making you the latest heart throb, and you will have millions of fans swooning at your feet. You'll travel everywhere in a big black limousine and have orange soda served to you in super-fancy glasses.

Well . . . um, OK, maybe your only fans will be the kids that live on your block, and you'll still travel on your bicycle, and still have to drink milk because Mom doesn't like you drinking orange soda all day. But it'll still be cool.

Anyway, the Rhythm and Poos is all about control, and being able to deliver the "two-cheek sneak" at just the right time in a song (when a little homemade percussion is needed). Fire up your streaming music account, search for any song by the old blues master "Muddy Underpants," and turn up the speakers as loud as they'll go.

Let Muddy play the *Dow dow dow dow dow* part, and then you follow it with perfectly formed (and timed) *poot poot poot poot poot!* Ah, the sweet smell of rhythm!

THE SNOW SHOVEL BUBBLE

Snow days are frequently ruined by my mom's horrible cry of "Milooo . . . can you shovel the driveway before someone falls on it?"

This spoils the fun in two ways—first, I've waited all year for the white stuff to arrive, and now Mom wants me to get rid of it. And second, shoveling is super-hard work! So I developed a special fart just for this occasion . . . a fart so unique that Snow-Shovels-R-Us should be offering us millions of dollars to can these babies and sell them as the best snow-clearing device of the millennium!

Here's how it works: first, you have to develop a taste for your grandma's fruitcake (I know, right?). It's a sacrifice worth making, because all that dried fruit creates the absolute *BEST* snow-clearing farts known to man! As luck would have it, we always get tons of fruitcakes delivered to our house for Christmas. Perfect!

After you've eaten as many fruitcakes as you possibly can, you're prepared for just about anything. Then, when Mom opens up the front door and hollers at you to go get the shovel, you'll simply stroll over to the driveway. Then, unzip your snow pants, point your butt wherever you want to blast a clear path, and let the fruitcake farts do the dirty work for you.

As it propels you along the drive at warp speed, the fruity fog will literally melt the snow behind you. So Mom gets the path cleared and you get some jet-propelled fun!

THE TRASH BUSTER

I love my mom, I really do. But she's a pretty bad cook, and sometimes I take so long to eat what's on my plate that Mom gets fed up with me and walks out of the kitchen. Perfect.

Eating Mom's burnt dinner specials are actually a double-edged sword for a farting prodigy like me. On the one hand, it's literally fuel for the fire—because the worse the food is, the stinkier my farts are. On the other hand, I'm just a ten-year-old kid and I think eating is pretty important to my survival! So here's how I've learned how dispose of a less-than-stellar dinner entrée without hurting my mom's feelings: I quietly open the trash, slide my food into it, lay some other garbage on top, and then fart into the trash can.

When Mom comes back into the kitchen, she will always check the garbage to make sure I haven't thrown away my dinner away (she's on to me!). But as soon as she opens the lid, the gassy guff—which has been festering for anything up to half an hour—shoots right up into her face and stings her eyes so bad she can't see. Then I rush to her aid, taking the garbage outside to empty it into the trash can. I get a 'Son of the Year' award for helping Mom and she never knows I haven't eaten my dinner!

DENTIST DEATH BREATH

If you're as scared of the dentist as I am, then you understand exactly what I mean when I say that just the thought of going for a dumb tooth cleaning makes my stomach stink up instantly. For days beforehand, my belly's tied up in knots and I can't eat, which means there is even more room for gas.

But the last time I went to get my pearly whites checked out, something happened to me that completely changed the way I feel about visiting the dentist. It all started as an accident, really. As the dentist came towards me with some scary looking shiny tools, I completely lost control of my butt cheeks and a foul-smelling fart escaped from my body in a long, sad-sounding *PPPPffftttttt*.

At first, he couldn't believe what he'd heard. Then his eyes started watering and he stumbled backward away from the chair, taking his tray of instruments with him! When I sat up in the seat, I could see that my dentist was out cold in the corner of the office and it looked like he'd peed his pants, too!

THE ATCHOO-POOT

Fun Fact: A sneeze comes out at around one hundred miles per hour! That is so awesome! So when you feel a sneeze coming on and you also have a back draft brewing, you know you're in for a double eruption of epic proportions! There is no way to hold on to the butt sneeze, if your nose is about to explode.

This is what we call the "Atchoo-Poot." A fart so fast, so furious, that it matches the velocity of the sneeze and comes shooting out of your butt in one ferocious blast. And because the force behind it is so strong, it all comes out in one go— short, sharp, and super smelly. It's even more fun if you are a multiple-sneezer; each fart gets quieter and quieter as you run out of gas. And the best part is, the sound of your fart is hidden by the noise of the sneeze, so you can lay the blame on someone else.

THE GHOST FART

Most times you can stick around to see the end results of your pooting: the gagging, the heaving, the nudging in the ribs. But with the Ghost Fart, you have to leave it to your imagination and trust that your floating air biscuit will do you proud.

All you need is a gurgling stomach and an elevator. It might involve a few rides up and down, so you need patience. And to be able to drop one on demand.

So, you get into an elevator and wait until it's empty. Then you start brewing. You wait until someone gets in and you walk out, depositing a stink bomb as you go, so that the doors close, trapping the person in the elevator along with the super pooper. If you're really quick you might be able to run up or down the stairs to the next level just in time to see them stumbling out, hand over their mouth, and looking for the nearest bin to barf in.

BLAME GAME GUFFS

This one is even more fun than the Ghost Fart. It's basically the same, but you need a few people to get in at the same time. You leave the elevator, depositing an almighty fizzler as you go, and the people inside will all be blaming the next person—looking at each other suspiciously and moving away from each other.

This one is solely responsible for the amount of people you see taking the stairs instead of the elevator—they just can't take the stench.

THE MUTT BUTT

In our house, it's each man (or dog) for himself when it comes to choosing a comfy seat to watch TV. Nine times out of ten, when I get home from school, my dog Pooter is already sprawled out on the couch, taking up all three seats and leaving nowhere for me to sit. My little sister Brittney always bags the armchair, so I either have to sit on the floor or squeeze in next to Pooter. After sitting on hard school chairs all day, the last thing I want to be doing is sitting on the floor, so I end up shoving Pooter along so I can fit in at the end of the couch.

But I discovered a foolproof way of getting the couch all to myself. After a couple of minutes of sitting next to him, I will drop little hints about Pooter's bad tummy. Things like "Pooter, have you got a bad tummy, boy?" or "Man, your stomach is grumbling today, Pooter." Then, once I know Brittney has heard me, I will lift the butt cheek nearest Pooter and slip one out in his direction. After a moment or so, the smell will reach Brittney and she will automatically think it was Pooter, and I will send him out of the room in disgrace.

Then I get the entire couch to myself.

THE HUMAN WHOOPEE CUSHION

My best friend Farty McPhee and I love putting the blame on other people, which is why this particular foul howl works best when we're both around. Farty McPhee is the best "guff guru" I know (apart from me, of course), so things get really smelly when we get together.

This can be done in any situation—on a bus, at home, at a party, or at school; in fact, anywhere that Farty and I can sit down with an empty chair between us. We wait for someone to come along and as they sit down on the chair, one of us will let rip with the loudest gas blaster we can muster.

The person on the other side will look at them in disgust and shock and exclaim "Oh my gosh, that is *disgusting*," get up, and walk away. Everyone will look at the person who has just sat down, and then the one who *actually* farted will walk away, holding his nose and shaking his head.

We did it once at a family wedding, just as the bride sat down. The photo album is hilarious.

THE FOG HORN

Nothing produces flatulence quite like fear. It's lucky, really, because our thunder from down under has saved mine and my best friend Farty's life on more than occasion. One time, our families took us on vacation and Farty and I found ourselves stranded in this marshy wasteland, with alligators and trolls and invisible ninja-ogres, and a green mist so thick we couldn't see the end of our noses. *Sigh*, OK, it was a play park near the holiday condo, but whatever. It suddenly got really foggy and I couldn't see Farty anywhere.

I was really scared and I don't mind admitting it! It was so still and so silent that I could hear my own heart beating until eventually I heard a sound—a sound I recognized. It felt like I had my very own chemistry lab in the pit of my stomach when all of a sudden . . . I let out the biggest, loudest, most thunderous fart I had ever made. Birds flew from the invisible branches high up in the fog. Car alarms went off.

Farty followed the sound and made his way back to me. Best of all, panic had made my fart so hot that it burned away the fog, giving us a clear view all the way back to the apartment.

THE TODDLER TICKLER

Sometimes, when my Aunt Sheila Botticoff comes over to visit, she brings her little baby son. And guess who's always left in charge of entertainment? Yup, me, Milo Snotrocket.

"Just tickle him, Milo. He likes that." My Aunt tells me over and over. Well, tickling is boring, and even though I like little Frankie, the thought of spending hours tickling him makes me want to barf.

So, I devised a plan to keep little Frankie Botticoff amused while I still got to watch TV.

By slowly eating peanuts throughout the visit, I can keep up a steady stream of really gassy bubblers. Sitting with my butt against little Frankie's side, each bubbler sends ripples over his ribs, just like a tickle. He will giggle for five minutes, giving me time to eat another few peanuts and then brew up another one. I can sit through entire episodes of *Captain Fart Man* without once having to pay attention to him.

Aunt Sheila can never understand how Frankie can smell so bad without having pooped in his diaper—and he can't tell her.

My secret remains safe.

THE AFTER-BATH BLAT

This one will ruin your day. Seriously. I mean, OK, so us boys do love rolling around in the mud, pretending to be Captain Fart Man or the newest recruit to the Secret Order of the Fart Ninjas, but secretly, we like to take baths, right?

So we sneak in a pinch of Mom's fancy-schmancy bath salts and we soak in the tub, pretending the fizzing fancy stuff is a ticking time bomb, ready to explode, and it is down to us to save the world from eternal destruction! But then it stops being all fizzy and we get out of the tub, all clean and fresh.

And then, just as we have one leg over the edge of the tub, out it comes . . . without warning . . . a big, wet, loud fart. And because we haven't dried ourselves off yet, the gas vibrates between our butt cheeks with a kind of "wet fish" flapping sound. As the stench is carried by the hot steam, it swirls around our heads, making our hair smell like butt.

THE SWIMMING POOL POOPER

There's a dilemma which affects every boy in our grade, every summer. And it all takes place at The Pool Party.

Every year, I have to go to Bobby Buttzcratcher's birthday party, and it always involves eating cowboy casserole and swimming. For those of you who don't know, Bobby's favorite food is a casserole made with sausages—and beans. Baked beans. The makers-of-all-things-fartish. And every year, we have to eat it, because if we don't, Bobby will dunk our heads in the pool. It's not that I don't like Cowboy Casserole as such, just not when I have to wear these stupid shorts which Mom insists on buying me every year.

The thing is, they are tight around the bottom of the leg, but baggy everywhere else. "Growing room," Mom calls it. Me, I call it a "gas bag" because when you fart in a pair of these things they hold it all in and they grow bigger and bigger, and your legs look fatter and fatter. You become a human flotation device. Until you jump out of the pool on to the side and then *Paaaarrrrpppp* . . . the force of you sitting down makes the gas escape. Loudly. In front of the parents. And because there is so much wet material flapping around, it actually sounds like you've followed through.

Gah, next year I'm going to make sure I'm sick.

THE UPHILL
BUTT SPILL

BLAT!

There are a lot of hills around near where I live. Not huge ones, but big enough to get in the way of my second (bet you can guess my first!) favorite pastime: cycling. Whenever Farty McPhee and I have any spare time, we drag our bikes out of the garage and head off with whatever food we can persuade Mom to give us.

Luckily, Farty and I have found a way to get up those hills without even being out of breath. As we approach the bottom of a hill, we stand up on the pedals and with all our might we push our biggest bean-bombers out, which propels us up the hill faster than anyone could ever pedal. It's like having our own personal jet packs attached to the saddle.

Once we've found a good spot to sit down and eat, we spread all our food out on the ground and pick the most fart-worthy ones to eat first. This gives the pickles and eggs time to fester in our stomachs for the return journey. Then, when we're full and our bellies are nicely gurgling, we set off back home, with our pickle-fueled farts ready to burst into action once more.

Whoever said that exercise was hard?

BASKETBALL
BOUNCERS

THBBBTF

I'm short. People have a habit of patting me on the head, like they do to my dog Pooter. So when it comes to playing basketball, I'm a little behind. But I don't *have* a little behind, which makes it great for farting!

Farting is one of the most useful skills you can master if you are lacking in height when it comes to shooting hoops. You have to compete with all the lanky boys, so you need to have something in your sports-related toolkit. Luckily for me, what I lack in height I make up for in flatulence.

As with many of my other guff-related skills, I discovered this one by accident, when I had the ball and was trying to score. I was so nervous that with every dribble of the ball I was letting one go—*bounce, poot, bounce, poot.* But as I went in for the final jump, a massive methane monster escaped. I shot six feet in the air and slam-dunked that ball right in the basket.

The guys hoisted me up on their shoulders (but quickly put me back down again because, well, I smelled) but I am never the last to be picked anymore!

CAMP FIRE FLAMER

Every year, my family and I go camping. We set up the tent and then sit around while Dad tries to build a fire to cook our supper on. It starts off with all of us excited, but by the time an hour has passed, Mom is opening bags of potato chips to keep us from dying of hunger, Brittney is falling asleep, and Mom is thinking longingly of her microwave oven at home.

This is where I come in. As Dad lights another match and puts it to the wood, I turn my back on the proceedings and push one out in the general direction of the match. That's all it takes. One fart and the fire is roaring, Mom is cheering, Dad is puffing his chest out because he thinks he's lit the fire, and I get to eat. It's a win-win situation

Mind you, I've had to be careful with the direction of the wind—the REAL wind I mean, because Dad really didn't look good the year the flame singed his eyebrows off.

THE FART ALARM

They say you can't smell your own farts, right? And it's true. Except when they're *really* strong, I can smell them then, but I've grown kinda fond of my old butt burps.

However, just because they don't make me gag doesn't mean other people are quite as accepting!

I discovered that, no matter where I hid it, my little sister Brittney would find my stash of candy. But she's only little, and Mom wouldn't tell her off. So I had to come up with a dastardly plan.

I put my goodies in one of my drawers and filled jars with my best farts—the really chewy ones that stick to things. Then I carefully placed the jars next to the candy, laid sheets of paper on top of the jars to keep the smell in, and slowly slid the drawer closed.

Brittney only tried once more after that. She's not very careful, so when she opened the drawer, the paper flew off the jars, releasing day-old gas right into her face!

Mom said you could hear the screaming from down the street. I don't even notice the smell, so now my stash is safe from everyone but me.

THE SONIC BOOM

This is a truly memorable fart—and it will stun all living creatures within a fifty-mile radius. I saved the Sonic Boom for last in this book, because it's one of the top secret weapons being developed by an astronomically top secret team of scientists commissioned by the International Society of Fart Enthusiasts.

In fact, most of our profits from selling poo perfume door-to-door go to the research fund for the Sonic Boom. It's the ultimate defense weapon, not just for the ISFE, but for the nation at large, and possibly the entire planet.

Due to the confidential nature of the project, however, this is all I can disclose: it involves airtight capsules that preserve and amplify the stinkiest farts from far and wide, in some of the most isolated regions in the world. This top-secret amplification technology will make the Sonic Boom our greatest safeguard against dangers, of which I'm not at liberty to speak (hint: space aliens). And guess what? I've made a special contribution to the project: my very own super stinky signature Snotrocket zinger, a specimen as disgusting as anything.